Colour CRACKERS

Read all the Colour CRACKERS books!

1 84121 244 X

1 84121 242 3

1 84121 232 6

1 84121 252 0

1 84121 258 X

1 84121 250 4

1 84121 228 8

1 84121 240 7

1 84121 238 5

1 84121 248 2

1 84121 256 3

1 84121 236 9

1 84121 246 6

1 84121 230 X

1 84121 234 2

1 84121 254 7

We Want William!

The Wisest Worm in the World!

Rose Impey
Shoo Rayner

ORCHARD BOOKS

ORCHARD BOOKS

96 Leonard Street, London EC2A 4XD

Orchard Books Australia

32/45-51 Huntley Street, Alexandria, NSW 2015

First published in Great Britain in 1995

This edition published in hardback in 2002

This edition published in paperback in 2003

Text © Rose Impey 1995

Illustrations © Shoo Rayner 2002

The rights of Rose Impey to be identified as the author
and Shoo Rayner as the illustrator of this work
have been asserted by them in accordance with the
Copyright, Designs and Patents Act, 1988.

A CIP catalogue record for this book is
available from the British Library.

ISBN 1 84121 876 6 (hardback)

ISBN 1 84121 256 3 (paperback)

1 3 5 7 9 10 8 6 4 2 (hardback)

3 5 7 9 10 8 6 4 (paperback)

Printed in China

We Want William!

William was a worm.
A very wise old worm.
The wisest worm in the world.
If worms had a problem
they couldn't work out,
they went to William.

"Wise William will know," they said.
"William will work it out."

"What William doesn't know
isn't worth knowing."
That's what worms told each other.

When a worm baby had measles

or mumps

or ate maggots,

Blurg!

their mums took them to William.

Come along!

9

When teenage worms wouldn't wash

or wouldn't work

or went all weepy,

their dads warned them,

We'll take you to William!

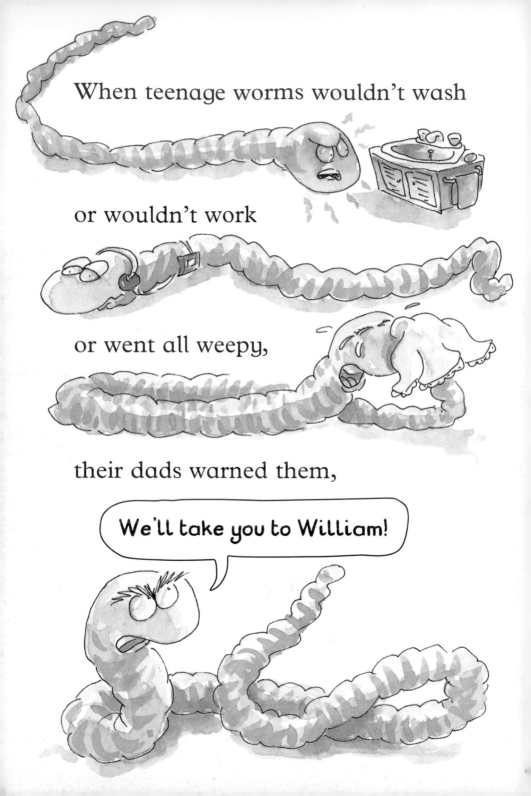

When the weather was too wet
or too warm,
and gangs of young worms ran wild,
older worms asked themselves,
"What would William do?"

One day William woke
to find some worms from
Wiggleton waiting to see him.
They had a terrible problem.
It was the worst story
William had ever heard.

The worms lived in the ground
under a school field;
Wiggleton Junior School field.
Sometimes, in the winter,
there were football matches
and snowball fights.

In the summer,
there were sports days
and school fêtes.
"We don't mind," said the worms.
"We're not complaining."

But once a year something
terrible happened.
It was so bad it made the
worms weep to talk about it.
"It's The World
Worm Charming Championship
we're worried about," they said.

"It happens in July.
People come to Wiggleton
from all over the world.
Hundreds of them,"
the worms told him.

"They come in their wellingtons,
with their wheelbarrows
and their windmills.
And their *secret weapons*."

"What sort of weapons?"
asked William.
The Wiggleton worms
lowered their voices to a whisper.
"All sorts of weapons," they said.

"Some we call 'Pokers'.
They try to poke us out.

They use garden forks

and cricket stumps

. and knitting needles.

They broggle about with
the ends of umbrellas.
We'd like to broggle *them*
with an umbrella
and see how they like it."

"Some we call 'Thumpers'.
They bang about above our heads

with lump hammers

and wooden spoons

and paddles.

They stamp their feet
and call it 'tap dancing'!
We'd like to tap dance
on *their* heads
and see how they like it."

"And some we call 'Charmers'.
They play music.

They sing songs.

They make up spells
and funny smells.
They try every trick in the book."

"And the trouble is, William,
some of them work.
Hundreds of worms wiggle-waggle
up to the surface.
The minute they put out
their heads, fingers grab them.
Whoosh!
But they still go
and the rest follow.
They're worse than lemmings!"

"What makes the humans do it?"
asked William. "What's it for?"

"For fun! For sport!
To see who can get the most,"
said the Wiggleton worms.
"Five hundred and eleven,
that's the record.

The fact is,
they set the worms free afterwards!
Those that survive.
But they're never the same again.
It's a terrible shame.
What's to be done, William?
That's what we want to know."

William was very old
and he was very wise,
but William had never heard
anything as bad as this before.

Over the next few weeks
all the worms in Wiggleton
heard about the campaign.

In schools young worms learned
how to recognise the enemy.
They learned what to do on
W-W-C-C Day.

Wiggleton worms joined
keep-fit classes

and body-building classes

and self-defence classes.

And every night,
deep in the dark, dark earth,
worms met in burrows,
to train in special *secret* units.
It was all hush-hush
and very (Sshh!) *secret*.

At last the big day came.
Every worm in Wiggleton was ready.
The very young worms
and the very old worms
were taken to a safe place
deep in the ground.
The other worms went
to join their groups,
ready for the battle.

REST
ROOM

NURSERY

On the school field
people were arriving
in cars and vans and buses.
They were carrying all sorts
of things with them,
all sorts of (Sshh!) *secret* weapons.

They were waiting for
the W-W-C-C to start.
Under the ground,
right under their feet,
the worms of Wiggleton
were ready too.

The whistle blew
and they were off.
The Pokers poked,
the Thumpers thumped,
and the Charmers started charming.
The Wiggleton Worms went wild.

An army of super-fit worms
worked against the Pokers.
They sawed off cricket stumps.

They nobbled knitting needles.

They grabbed hold of garden forks.

They even poked the odd 'Poker',
just to see how *he* liked it.

Ow!

Heave!

A band of brave worms
wearing hard hats
and carrying spades
gave the Thumpers a fright.
They soon put a stop
to their tap dancing!

And the rest of the worms
showed the Charmers
they had a few tricks of their own.

No one could believe their eyes.
They had never seen
anything like it.
The worms were escaping
as fast as they were being caught.

Everyone started falling out.
There were more accidents
and arguments
and fights
than after a football match.

Everyone went home worn out.
"Never again."
"What a wash-out."
"Too dangerous," they said.

Under the ground,
right under their feet,
the Wiggleton worms
were worn out too.
But they were happy
and victorious worms.

"We want William," they cried.
"Three cheers for William.
Hip, hip, hooray!
Hip, hip, hooray!
Hip, hip, hooray!!!"

Crack-A-Joke

How can you tell a worm's head from its tail?
Tickle it in the middle and see which end smiles!

What's round and bad-tempered?
A vicious circle!

WAITER! What's this worm doing in my soup?

Drowning, Sir.

HELP!

What's worse than finding a worm in an apple?
Finding half a worm!

What's long, pink and fluffy?
A worm in a pink angora jumper!

Did you know that bookworms can eat through five chapters a week!

A BARREL OF LAUGHS by JOE KING

DANGEROUS WALKS by CLIFF EDGE

HOW TO AVOID ACCIDENTS by LUKE OUT

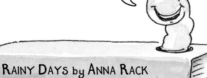

RAINY DAYS by ANNA RACK

A LIFE OF CRIME by ROBIN BANKS

JUMBO JETS by ELLIE FANT

There are 16 Colour Crackers books.
Collect them all!

❏ A Birthday for Bluebell   1 84121 228 8   £3.99

❏ A Fortune for Yo-Yo   1 84121 230 X   £3.99

❏ A Medal for Poppy   1 84121 244 X   £3.99

❏ Hot Dog Harris   1 84121 232 6   £3.99

❏ Long Live Roberto   1 84121 246 6   £3.99

❏ Open Wide, Wilbur   1 84121 248 2   £3.99

❏ Phew, Sidney!   1 84121 234 2   £3.99

❏ Pipe Down, Prudle!   1 84121 250 4   £3.99

❏ Precious Potter   1 84121 236 9   £3.99

☑ Rhode Island Roy   1 84121 252 0   £3.99

☑ Sleepy Sammy   1 84121 238 5   £3.99

❏ Stella's Staying Put   1 84121 254 7   £3.99

❏ Tiny Tim   1 84121 240 7   £3.99

☑ Too Many Babies   1 84121 242 3   £3.99

❏ We Want William!   1 84121 256 3   £3.99

❏ Welcome Home, Barney   1 84121 258 X   £3.99

Colour Crackers are available from all good bookshops,
or can be ordered direct from the publisher:
Orchard Books, PO BOX 29, Douglas IM99 1BQ
Credit card orders please telephone 01624 836000 or fax 01624 837033
or e-mail: bookshop@enterprise.net for details.
To order please quote title, author and ISBN and your full name and address.
Cheques and postal orders should be made payable to 'Bookpost plc'.
Postage and packing is FREE within the UK
(overseas customers should add £1.00 per book).
Prices and availability are subject to change.

1 84121 244 X

1 84121 240 7

1 84121 238 5

1 84121 252 0

1 84121 256 3

1 84121 236 9

1 84121 228 8

1 84121 230 X

1 84121 234 2

1 84121 248 2

1 84121 242 3

1 84121 232 6

1 84121 246 6

1 84121 258 X

1 84121 250 4

1 84121 254 7

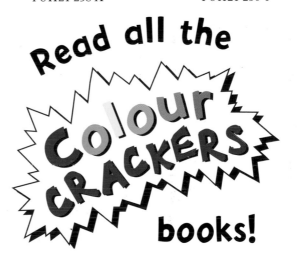

Read all the **Colour CRACKERS** books!

Collect all the
Colour Crackers!